Capitol Hill Library

NO LONGER PROPERTY OF
SEATTLE PUBLIC LIBRARY

Grand Jeté and Me

Written by ALLEGRA KENT • *Illustrated by* ROBIN PREISS GLASSER

HARPER
An Imprint of HarperCollins*Publishers*

For my dear grandchildren, with love—
Miranda, Georgia, Shane, and Peyton
—AK

To Allegra, who inspired me as a young
dancer and to all who witnessed her magic.
—RPG

Grand Jeté and Me
Text copyright © 2021 by Allegra Kent
Illustrations copyright © 2021 by Robin Preiss Glasser
All rights reserved. Manufactured in Italy.
No part of this book may be used or reproduced in any manner whatsoever without written
permission except in the case of brief quotations embodied in critical articles and reviews.
For information address HarperCollins Children's Books, a division of HarperCollins Publishers,
195 Broadway, New York, NY 10007.
www.harpercollinschildrens.com

ISBN 978-0-06-239202-2

The artist used micron pen, watercolor, and gouache on Arches watercolor paper
to create the illustrations for this book.
Typography by Jeanne Hogle
21 22 23 24 25 RTLO 10 9 8 7 6 5 4 3 2 1
❖
First Edition

I'm going to visit my grandmother. She is not like other grandmothers. I don't call her Grandma or Nana or Abuela. I call her Grand Jeté.

My grandmother was once a prima ballerina—that's the fanciest kind of ballerina of all. She danced on stages all over the world. She never stopped dancing.

I love to visit her in her apartment in New York, especially at Christmastime.

"Come in!" says Grand Jeté as she opens the door wide. "Make your entrance, my beautiful granddaughter!"

I chassé into her hallway
and she applauds for me.
I curtsy.

“I’m delighted to see you, my darling,” says Grand Jeté. She doesn’t talk like other grandmothers, either. “Shall we have a little lunch before we go?”

“Yes, please!” I say. I love lunch with Grand Jeté. She always makes it special.

"Follow me," she says. "Straight spine, please, my sweetheart."

I follow her back to the kitchen. I have been practicing my ballet steps all week to get ready.

When we make lunch,
we arabesque our plates

and lunge for
the milk.

We plié next to the stools before we sit down.

We sit at the counter and unfold our napkins.

"Spine straight!" says Grand Jeté. I sit up even straighter. "Perfect!" she says, and she gives me a big squeeze.

After lunch comes my favorite part. “Let’s put on our faces,” says Grand Jeté. My grandmother is the only person I know with a vanity and a dressing room.

“Ready?” asks Grand Jeté.

"Ready," I say. I turn on the switch. Her mirror lights up! There are a hundred bulbs all around it. At least it looks like a hundred bulbs.

"First our hair," says Grand Jeté. She pulls her hair back from her face and sweeps it up in a bun.
Then she does mine.

"Now our eyes," says Grand Jeté. She puts a great big swash of makeup on her eyes and they get huge. Then she puts a little swash of makeup on my eyes and they get bigger, too.

"And now, a little polish," says Grand Jeté. She makes her lips dark red. She gives my lips a little gloss.

Finally, we put on the holiday outfits that Grand Jeté got for us today. Our big day.

“And now, I think we are ready,” Grand Jeté says.

We take the elevator down, down, down to the ground floor. "Look!" says Grand Jeté. "A barre!"

We nod to the doorman and then we hurry along the sidewalk. I know exactly where we're going. And I can't wait.

We bow to the
woman selling hats.

And buy a bouquet
of roses at the market.
Grande Jeté does
not play softball. Or
volleyball. She doesn't
even bowl.

But she knows how to throw flowers. "Toss them just like this," Grand Jeté says to me. "Underhand and softly."

I've done this before. I do it just right. The people on the street give us funny looks. We just smile and bow.

When we arrive at the theater, I'm so excited.
I do a grand jeté, which is a big leap.

Then we hurry through
the backstage door to
greet Grand Jeté's friends.

Everyone here knows Grand Jeté! But they call her Madame. She is famous!

"I'll be dancing the ballerina role—Sugar Plum Fairy—the one your grandmother used to dance," says one of the dancers.

We rush to our seats. Soon *The Nutcracker* will begin!

Grand Jeté says, “The ballet begins on Christmas Eve, with a party at the home of a little girl, Marie, and her family.”

I hold Grand Jeté’s hand when Marie’s godfather, Drosselmeyer, gives her the Nutcracker doll.

But her naughty brother breaks it. When the party is over, Marie falls asleep with her broken doll.

She is awakened by flashing lights. The Christmas tree grows, and all the toys, including Marie's Nutcracker, become life-size. Giant mice attack her.

The mice and a terrible seven-headed Mouse King battle the Nutcracker and his soldiers.

Marie throws her shoe at the Mouse King, and the Nutcracker kills him. The battle is won.

Marie's Nutcracker turns into a prince who takes her on a magical journey.

Marie and the Prince
walk through a forest, and
it snows right on stage.

They travel to the Land of Sweets, where they are entertained by the whole kingdom.

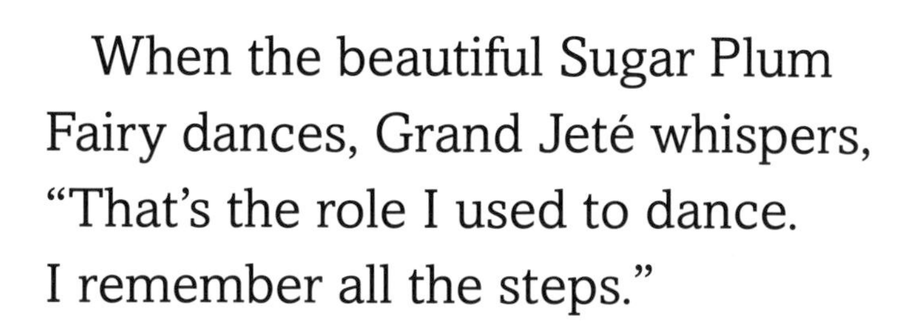

When the beautiful Sugar Plum Fairy dances, Grand Jeté whispers, “That’s the role I used to dance. I remember all the steps.”

At the end everyone waves as Marie and the Prince fly home in a sleigh. I wave, too.

Was it all a dream?

The curtain closes and we jump to our feet and clap and clap.

The prima ballerina takes a final bow and smiles right at Grand Jeté. I toss up the flowers, just the way Grand Jeté showed me.

She blows us a kiss. We blow a kiss back.

“She’s a prima ballerina, Grand Jeté!” I say. “You were just like her.” Grand Jeté smiles. She blows a final kiss to the stage, but the curtain has already come down.

“I was just like her, my darling,” she says. “And someday you might be, too.”

She picks up our programs and heads to the aisle.
"Ready to rumble?" she asks.
"Ready to rumble," I say.
And together we waltz out of the theater.

A NOTE FROM ALLEGRA KENT

When they were very young, I took my granddaughters to see New York City Ballet's signature production of *The Nutcracker*, choreographed by George Balanchine. The girls had been told the story of how I had been a ballerina and that I had even danced in the very same *Nutcracker* they were about to enjoy. I could see their delight as they were treated to the magic of the beautiful sets, costumes, and music but also imagining their grandmother in the role of the Sugar Plum Fairy. A feeling of nostalgia swept over me as I realized that, although the world changes, *The Nutcracker* endures.

In 1954, two years after I joined the company at age fifteen, Balanchine created his version of *The Nutcracker*. He borrowed from the nineteenth century E. T. A. Hoffmann libretto, which I describe in this book. The heroine is called Marie, instead of the Americanized Clara; Drosselmeyer is Marie's godfather in his version, not her uncle.

As they have thrilled millions at Lincoln Center for over sixty-five years, we still see the lush costumes by Karinska and sets by Rouben Ter-Arutunian illustrated in this book by Robin Preiss Glasser.

Every year during the Christmas season, professional and suburban companies and schools around the world perform *The Nutcracker*. They all use the iconic music by Peter Ilyich Tchaikovsky.

This book is my way of celebrating the joy I felt while dancing *The Nutcracker* and so many other ballets for thirty years with New York City Ballet and to thank Mr. B, as we called him, for his enormous gift to the generations of children—and their parents and grandparents—who discover and rediscover this ballet.

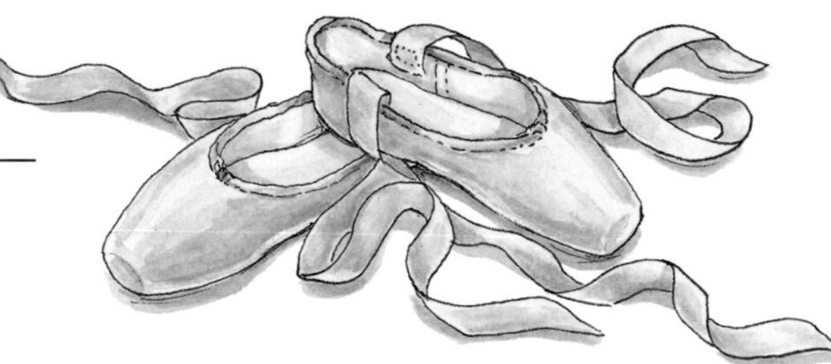

GLOSSARY OF TERMS:

Grand Jeté: a big leap with legs extended

Prima Ballerina: a term usually reserved for the top female dancers in the world

Ballerina: a female principal dancer in a ballet company

Chassé: a chasing step

Arabesque: a pose on one leg with the other extended behind

Plié: a bend of the legs with knees to the side

Barre: a railing that dancers use for support at the beginning of a ballet class

Curtsy: a bow that the women dancers perform at the end of a ballet or variation

Madame: a title of respect used in speaking to an older woman, especially one of distinction

Waltz: a dance in three quarter time, sometimes performed with a partner